THE FORMULA FOR TROUBLE

Megan Stine & H. William Stine

ILLUSTRATIONS BY DAVID FEBLAND

SCHOLASTIC INC.
New York Toronto London Auckland Sydney Tokyo

For Cody:
The plot has thickened since your arrival.
M&D

ISBN 0-590-32638-4

 Published by Scholastic Inc.

13 12 11 10 9 8 7 6 5 4 3 4 5 6 7/8

Printed in the U.S.A. 01

BEWARE!!!
DO NOT READ THIS BOOK FROM BEGINNING TO END

You are about to sample a portion of the most unpredictable potion you will ever drink. One sip of this fantastic brew will make you a new person. It may even make an animal out of you!

You will have adventures you have never experienced before, but *only* if you follow the directions at the bottom of each page. A wrong turn can mean danger or even death! The right one could give you the most fun you have ever had.

What happens depends on you. If you get into trouble, turn back and choose a different way out. If you're having a good time, keep going!

So be daring and take a sip of this miracle formula. Bottoms up!

Now turn to PAGE 2.

One sunny Saturday afternoon in the middle of May you get a phone call from your friend Mr. Watson, the chemistry teacher. "I've done it! I've really done it this time," he says. "You're not going to believe your own eyes. Get over here as fast as you can!"

You are on your bike in a flash. Sure, Mr. Watson has said it before — and he was wrong! Like the time he thought he had discovered a great new mouthwash, but all it did was turn one ear red and one ear green. Or the time he was sure he had discovered a new cream to prevent sunburn, but all he had done was reinvent poison ivy.

But maybe this time will be different. You jump off your bike and ring his front doorbell, but no one answers. So you head straight for the homemade laboratory he built in his garage.

The door to the lab is closed, and you knock, saying, "Okay, Mr. Watson, I'm ready to not believe my own eyes!" But still no one answers. You press your ear to the door; nothing is bubbling, boiling, or humming. "Hey, Mr. Watson," you call, "what's the joke?" That's when you discover that the door is unlocked. You go in.

If you want your dog to go in with you, turn to PAGE 4.

If you want to go in alone, turn to PAGE 6.

If you want a friend to go in with you, turn to PAGE 10.

As you turn the doorknob, your faithful dog Titanic jumps on the door, and it swings open. Mr. Watson is nowhere to be seen.

"You pick the strangest times for playing hide-and-seek, Mr. Watson," you say with a laugh. "Okay, Titanic, go find Mr. Watson."

Titantic barks twice and runs immediately to a small closet in the corner of the garage. You open the closet quickly and twenty-five old golf clubs fall down on you. But other than that, the closet is empty. Titanic is a faithful dog, but you've got to face facts — he's the worst bloodhound in the fifty states.

Convinced now that Mr. Watson isn't in the lab, you look around on your own. That's when you see his notebook, the secret one he always keeps locked up, lying on a table. Your eyes open wide as you read the entry written earlier that morning:

> Mankind has always dreamed about superhuman physical strength in movies and comic books. I am on the verge of making that dream a reality. Six months of tedious and tireless work have paid off. I am about to drink my latest invention and then experience what no man on this earth has experienced before. But first, I'm hungry. I'm going out for a burger. More later.

Go on to PAGE 5.

"Wow," you say out loud as though Titanic actually understands what you say. As you close the notebook, you see a small, clear glass beaker with a label written in Mr. Watson's handwriting: SUPER-STRENGTH POTION. NO ARTIFICIAL COLORS OR FLAVORS.

"I wonder what it would be like to be the strongest person in the world, Titanic," you say, staring at the clear liquid.

If you decide to drink the potion, turn to PAGE 21.

If you decide not to, turn to PAGE 13.

Mr. Watson isn't in the lab, so you sit down to catch your breath after your long, tiring bike ride. If you could only find something to drink, the bike ride home would be a lot easier. This lab looks like the Hall of Fame of Bungled Experiments. There are parrot pills, for example — pills guaranteed to make your parrot talk. Well, they worked, sort of. Every bird that tried one said the words "I'm dying" clearly and distinctly right before it fell off its perch.

Then there was Mr. Watson's fire extinguisher. Another winner. It put out fires by spraying the blaze with a gas that gave people hiccups for two weeks.

"Aha! Mr. Watson has finally come up with something I really need," you say to yourself, seeing a glass of water sitting on a table. Wiping your sweaty forehead with one hand, you reach for the glass with the other.

If you drink the water, turn to PAGE 25.

If you don't drink the water, go to PAGE 33.

If you clumsily knock over the glass, spilling the water all over everything, don't bother to wipe up the mess. Go directly to PAGE 34!

One of the thugs has his hands around your throat, and he's lifting you off the ground. You barely gasp out the words: "Wait a minute! There's more formula back at the lab." The thug, who doesn't make any decisions of his own, looks at Von Ranier first. When Von Ranier nods his head, the hands around your neck loosen.

"More formula, my young friend?" Von Ranier asks you again.

"A little . . . but enough for you to analyze and figure out the formula," you say.

Mr. Watson's face shows mixed emotions: he's happy to be alive; but unhappy about your plan. In the back of the car, as you drive back to Mr. Watson's garage, he whispers to you, "I don't want you involved in this. It isn't safe."

Go on to PAGE 8.

"Don't worry," you whisper back. "I'm going to give them something to analyze that, when they drink it, will knock their ears off."

In the lab, a little while later, you go straight to a beaker that has a small puddle of black liquid on the bottom.

"Don't give them the formula!" Mr. Watson says, winking secretly to you.

"It's the only way to stay alive," you tell him, as you hand the beaker over to Von Ranier. "Here it is. Now leave us alone."

"We'll be glad to leave you alone . . . but there's one more small request I'd like to make," he says, pushing the beaker back toward you. "Drink it! Drink it now!!" And the two thugs pull their guns out again.

There's nothing written on the beaker label, and you don't have any idea what this stuff will do to you.

If you drink it, turn to PAGE 107.
If you don't drink it, go to PAGE 20.

As you look around campaign headquarters, you feel proud. As Titanic's handpicked . . . er, uh . . . paw-picked campaign manager, you have created his entire presidential campaign. Titanic's praise is a little more modest, of course. "I always knew you'd be good for something," he tells you as he surveys the posters, badges, bumper stickers, and press releases, all showing Titanic wearing a three-piece suit and his campaign button: "LET'S GET THE FAT CATS OUT OF WASHINGTON."

"It's all very impressive, but it won't do you any good," says a voice in the back of the room. Everyone turns and sees the sneering face of Rory Maltin, a sneaky and underhanded reporter for the *National Filth,* a thoroughly untrustworthy newspaper. Rory shouts, "I've got the goods on you, Titanic, and it looks as if you've been a bad dog," he says, patting his briefcase. "No one will vote for you after they read my story tomorrow."

However, Rory doesn't get to finish his threat because Titanic chases him out of the room. And when Titanic returns, you discover Rory Maltin's briefcase . . . the one with all the supposed scandal evidence.

If you decide to open the briefcase, go to PAGE 35.

If you think it's wrong to open it, go to PAGE 39.

"Hey, maybe we'd better wait for him outside," your friend suggests as you look into the empty laboratory.

"Don't be a chicken. I'm telling you, Mr. Watson is a great guy — a little strange, maybe, but a great guy," you explain.

"I just mean that historically this is a dumb thing to do. Remember Hansel and Gretel, Goldilocks, and Snow White? You can get into serious trouble going into strangers' houses," your friend still insists.

"This isn't a house. It's a garage. So we're safe, okay? Anyway, I'm sure he'll be here any second. He sounded really excited about showing me something."

"That's what the wolf said to Little Red Riding Hood," your friend says.

"What is this hangup you have with fairy tales today? You're making me crazy."

"Well, my father always told me that —"

"Hey, don't do that!" you shout.

Your friend is leaning against the shelves Mr. Watson always says need a warning sign that reads: DON'T EVER LEAN AGAINST THESE SHELVES. The shelves sway back and forth, and both of you watch a glass beaker with a thick, shiny green liquid lose its balance and fall.

If the green goop falls on you, go on to PAGE 11.

If you'd rather have it spill on your friend, go to PAGE 29.

Your friend gets up slowly. "Hey, you didn't have to push me so hard!"

"Yes, I did. That stuff was going to fall on you," you say.

"Hey, where are you?" your friend asks.

"I'm over here," you answer.

"Where?"

"Over here. Stop joking around and help me clean up this mess," you order.

"But I can't see you," your friend says. "Go look in the mirror. I think you've lost a little weight."

You go over to the mirror on the wall, and now you see what your friend sees — or doesn't see. You're invisible.

Just then the bell on a timer goes off and a tape recorder clicks on. It's Mr. Watson with a message for you. "On top of the shelves you'll find my latest experiment, which I have put up there for safekeeping. I thought I had discovered a chocolate fudge sauce with no calories. But after trying it on two sundaes, I realized instead that it makes people invisible. The potion must get to Professor Vaccas at the university. Obviously I can't take it there in my present condition, so I want you to do it for me. But be careful. I'll see you soon — as soon as you can see me. Thanks."

Go on to PAGE 12.

"Hey, you're back. I can see you again," your friend says.

"I guess the stuff wears off unless you eat it," you say. You start scraping the green stuff off the floor into a small jar. "Let's get over to the university before anything else happens," you suggest.

"What for?" Your friend suddenly has the glow of someone with an idea that never should have been thought of. "There's only a little left. Let's use it on ourselves."

If you decide to do what your friend wants, go to PAGE 22.

If you decide to do what Mr. Watson asked you to do, go on to PAGE 46.

Something in the back of your mind stops you from taking that drink. "What are the chances that Mr. Watson's latest formula really works?" you ask yourself. The answer is obvious: it's about as likely as your dentist telling you, "It's so nice out today, let's play catch instead of tightening your braces."

So you put the beaker down and look around the lab. Suddenly you hear a sound that makes you spin around. It's Titanic lapping away at the liquid in the beaker.

"Titanic! Don't drink that! Get down from there!" you shout.

Titanic lifts his head from the beaker, looks at you, and says, "You know, it doesn't taste bad once you get used to it."

You sit down in shock, even though there isn't a chair under you. "Titanic, did you just do what I think you did even though I know you can't, and I must be crazy for thinking you did?"

"Yes, and your grammar is atrocious," your dog informs you. "Almost as atrocious as the stuff you've been calling dog food and leaving in my bowl. I wouldn't feed that garbage to a cat."

"Mr. Watson, come here. I need you," you say with a shaking voice.

Go on to PAGE 14.

"And there are a few other changes I plan to make, buster," Titanic continues. "I want an electric blanket. No more of this sleeping on the floor. And forget about fetching, too. If you throw a stick and want it back, GET IT YOURSELF!"

"Titanic, would you shut up a minute? I've got to do some fast thinking," you say.

"From now on, I'll do the thinking around here," your dog tells you.

If you would like to even the score with Titanic, drink some of the formula yourself and go on to PAGE 75.

If you want to take orders from your dog for a change, go on to PAGE 15.

Ten minutes later you find yourself sitting next to your dog in Frosty's Ice Cream Parlor. Titanic insists on getting a hot butterscotch-and-marshmallow sundae under his belt.

"But you're not wearing a belt," you remind him.

"One more wise-guy remark like that, and I'll wash your mouth out with flea soap," Titanic says. "Don't you realize you're sitting next to a million bucks? All I have to do is figure out how to market my new talent."

"Okay, what will you — hey, no dogs allowed in here, kid," the waiter says.

"Bring me a hot butterscotch-and-marshmallow sundae with two cherries," Titanic says.

"Hey, how did you do that?" the waiter asks you.

"Don't ask me; ask my friend the chemistry teacher," you explain, although it doesn't clear up the question at all.

"Do I get my sundae, or do I have to bite you on the leg?" Titanic demands. Realizing that the dog really is talking, the waiter turns as white as his apron and disappears behind the counter.

Go on to PAGE 16.

He's back in a minute with the sundae. "Uh, that'll be seven dollars, please," the waiter says.

Licking marshmallow off his nose, Titanic tells you, "Pay him."

Glaring at your dog, you shell out seven bucks — all the money you have. The waiter puts it in his pocket with a smile. "You know," he says, "we don't get many dogs coming in here asking for an ice cream sundae."

Now, if you know the punch line to this old joke, turn to PAGE 89.

If you don't know it, turn to PAGE 104.

Politics? Who is he kidding? You can think of about a million good reasons why Titanic would be a lousy president, and if you had another second, you could think of about a million more.

But you know what? Who cares what you think!! You're the one who decided you wanted to take orders from your dog. So keep your mouth shut, and do what your dog tells you to do.

Now go to PAGE 9 like a good, obedient master before Titanic takes a newspaper to you.

What do you mean, *lucky*? Ha! Your luck ran out when you drank the formula and turned into a werewolf — which is what you are, in case you haven't figured it out yet.

"Yikes," you say to yourself, now that the whole horrible truth has been revealed to you.

You open the lab door and burst out, running directly into the two people you heard before. They turn out to be the school principal and a policewoman who have come to check on strange noises coming from Mr. Watson's lab or, more precisely, coming from *Mr. Watson* himself in the past few days.

The principal recognizes your bike and calls you by name, but you have just graduated *summa cum furry,* and you've got to get out of there!

But before you ride off in a cloud of hair, here's a decision you've got to make:

If you want to be a good werewolf, turn to PAGE 36.

If you want to be a bad one, turn to PAGE 38.

20

"Hey, I don't want to drink this. This isn't the right formula. I just said that as a joke," you explain with a weak laugh. "Come on, you guys, can't you take a joke?"

A sense of humor, however, is pretty high on Von Ranier's list of missing parts to his personality. He points at the two thugs, and they begin shooting without a second thought.

And in case you're thinking there's still a chance for the two of you to come through in this high-caliber story, we'll spell it out for you:

THE END

"Well, just a little of this super-strength potion can't hurt me. Besides, it's a long bike ride home, and I could use some strength for that," you tell yourself as you lift the beaker to your lips.

Titanic is scratching furiously on the floor, probably trying to dig a hole to hide in. "Calm down, Titanic. I'll only take a little sip," you explain. The liquid is thick and tastes like sugarless lemonade. "See, no big deal," you tell Titanic. But when you bend down to pet him, he takes one look at you and starts to growl. Then he races out the door as though a twelve-foot cat were chasing him.

"Hey! What's wrong with you, Titanic?" you call. That's when the first pain in your stomach hits you like a fast ball.

"Hey! What's wrong with me?????"

Go on to PAGE 25.

You and your friend stand facing each other, both a little afraid to drink the formula first. Finally you both agree it's down the hatch together, and suddenly you're not facing each other anymore.

"It works! Where'd you go?" your friend asks.

"Ouch! You're standing on my foot," you say.

"Ouch. Something hit my head," your friend says.

"That was *my* head," you explain, trying to find your sore forehead to rub it.

After a couple of minutes of banging into each other like Dodg'em cars, the two of you make it out the door. You already know where you're going — straight for the airport! You quickly realize that being invisible gives you a no-fair advantage: you'll never have to pay another plane fare again!

"We could listen in on all of the top secret meetings in Russia and China and become famous spies. No one could stop us," you say.

"Great plan . . . but there's one small problem: I can't speak Russian or Chinese, can you?"

"No," you remember.

Go on to PAGE 24.

Okay, so the two of you aren't cut out to be spies. But you both can have some fun while you're invisible. Your first stop is Washington, D.C., where you have dinner with the president, although he doesn't know you're there. Then you're off to Disneyland, where you ride everything for free. After that, it's rock concerts in L.A. where you mingle with the stars backstage; then shopping in New York department stores after they've closed; then you're on location where your favorite stars are filming movies; and finally you sit in the dugout during an All-Star baseball game. You have great seats, although a couple of players accidentally spit tobacco on you. Well, who said being invisible was trouble-free?

What's next?

If you've had enough and are homesick, go to PAGE 57.

If you want to keep traveling, go to PAGE 79.

Suddenly your skin starts itching. It feels as if a million ants are having a dance contest all over your body. You start breathing heavily because you're hot and then you're cold and then you're hot and cold at the same time. You're trying to ignore these effects, but the knot in your stomach is beginning to get a little scary. Worst of all, you feel so weak that you can hardly stand up. You stumble over a table, knocking Mr. Watson's experiment notebook to the floor. It takes all of your strength to bend down and pick it up. Then you notice that it has fallen open to the last entry, written just an hour ago. There are also two photographs pasted on the page. Here they are.

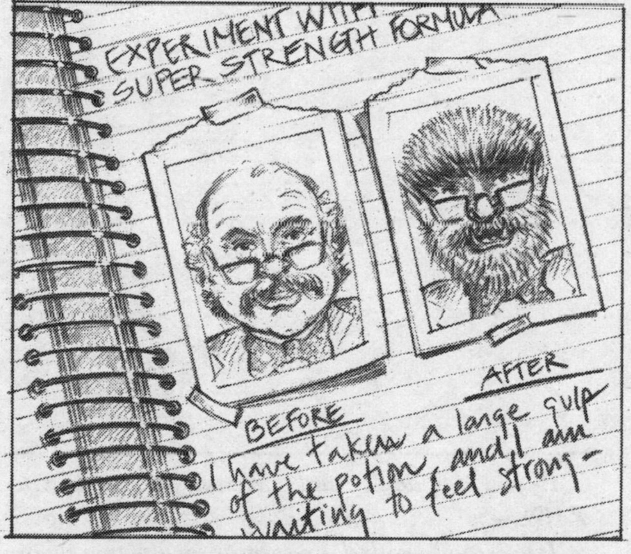

Go on to PAGE 26.

Seeing the photographs makes you jump back. You run to the mirror. You jump back again, this time in horror! Sure enough, you are covered with thick, red fur. Your ears are as pointed as your teeth. And your hands are grotesque paws as big as catchers' mitts.

"Mr. Watson — you blew it again!" you howl.

"What on earth was that?" says a voice outside.

"I think it came from inside the garage," another voice says. Then you hear footsteps coming your way.

What should you do?

If you decide to make a run for it, turn to PAGE 43.

If you look around the lab for an electric razor, turn to PAGE 51.

You dial the phone quickly, not knowing exactly what you're going to tell the CIA people. A friendly woman's voice answers, "Hello, CIA. We know everything."

"My friend Mr. Watson, the chemistry teacher, is a CIA agent," you say.

"Yes, we know that," the woman says, interrupting you.

"He was just kidnapped by two men with guns," you go on.

"Oh. We didn't know that. Stay where you are; we'll be right over," the woman says.

Before you can hang up the phone, the door opens and a man in a trench coat enters. You don't know who he is, so you don't say anything.

"Anybody in here? So Watson's been kidnapped, huh . . . hey, come on out. I know you're here. You phoned. There's no time to waste if you want to help Watson," the man says, taking a badge out of his pocket. He is Agent Murphy of the CIA.

"I'm right here, standing in front of you," you explain.

Agent Murphy looks right through you at the standing lamp behind you. "I knew Watson was working on something weird, but I didn't think it was a talking pole lamp," he says.

"I'm not a pole lamp. I'm Mr. Watson's friend, and I'm invisible. I drank Mr. Watson's latest experiment," you explain.

Go on to PAGE 28.

"Invisible . . . that's nice. Well, then, there's no time to lose. Whoever took him must know Watson was working on this formula, and they'll get pretty rough with him. They'll keep him alive for a while, but only for a while."

"What should we do?" you ask.

"I can't do anything. It's going to be up to you. You'll have to do some work for us — find something valuable enough for us to trade for Watson . . . something like a double agent, someone who's working for them while they're working for us. Listen closely. I've only got time to tell this to you once . . ."

Go on to PAGE 41.

You catch the glass beaker before it hits the ground, but some of the green liquid splashes on your friend. As it slowly drips down like a raw egg, your friend gradually disappears.

"I knew something like this was going to happen. I warned you," your friend says glumly. "What does Mr. Watson call this? The perfect spot remover?"

"He calls this his greatest discovery yet," you say, reading Mr. Watson's notebook. The page turns even though you aren't holding the book, and you know your friend is standing next to you reading Mr. Watson's last entry.

> I drank the formula twelve hours ago, and I am convinced of the permanence of my invisible state. I am ready to do something bold and reckless, something I've never attempted before in my life. I am going to see if I can sneak into the movies without paying. More later.

"That was three days ago," you say to your friend, who has suddenly popped back into sight and is standing by the beaker with the remaining green, syrupy liquid.

"What are you doing?" you ask.

"Mr. Watson has no imagination," your friend says. "I'm about to follow in the footsteps of the world's greatest scientists, Isaac Newton, Louis Pasteur, Dr. J."

Go on to PAGE 30.

"If you drink that stuff, no one will be able to follow your footsteps," you say.

"That's the idea," your friend says, gulping down the formula. Your friend is invisible in a second. "People always believe there's a logical explanation for everything that happens. Well, I'm going to shake them up a bit. I'm going to see what people do when there's an illogical explanation for what goes on. Besides that, now I have the perfect disguise for committing the perfect crime!"

You've got to stop your friend.

If you block the door, go to PAGE 49.

If you think it's easier to follow your friend, turn to PAGE 56.

Very clever of you to figure out that the midway point referred to the midway in an amusement park! And "Pharaoh's Wheel" was really the ferris wheel — either a garbled message, or Roberto was a terrible speller. (Of course, if you went to the Sphinx Motors instead, you found it closed. Fortunately, the amusement park was right across the street, and you probably got here in time.)

As you wander past the carousel and the ferris wheel for the sixth time, you realize this is a better place to hide someone than you first thought. But where could the two thugs be hiding Mr. Watson? Then you notice a man patrolling a booth that seems to be closed. Why would anyone need to guard a locked booth? That must be where the men are keeping Mr. Watson.

Since you're invisible, you have no trouble getting past the guard and into the booth. Once inside, you see that it's not a carnival booth at all but a complete science lab. And alone in the middle of the test tubes and chemicals is a very tired-looking Mr. Watson.

You walk up to him silently and whisper, "Don't worry. I'll get you out of here." You expect Mr. Watson to smile with relief when he hears your voice, but what he says surprises you. "What time is it, is it day or night?" he asks.

"What difference does that make? I'm going to get you out of this mess," you say.

Go on to PAGE 32.

"It's a matter of life and death — mine. Roberto sold information about me to these crazy terrorists. It's an organization of social rejects who turned to terrorist activities to get even with the world. I've stalled them as long as I can, but if I don't give them the formula *tonight,* they'll kill me when they get here. That's why I've got to know — what time is it?"

If you're reading this book during the day, go to PAGE 83.

If it's nighttime, close this book and go to sleep. You're too late to save Mr. Watson!

You put the glass down. For a minute, you almost forgot where you were. A chemistry lab is no place to sample unlabeled drinks!

You hear footsteps and turn to see Mr. Watson coming in.

"Boy, you just missed it. I almost did a really dumb thing," you tell him. "I was so hot and thirsty, I almost drank from this glass."

"I know. That's exactly what I expected you to do. But now you're spoiling my plan," Mr. Watson says, grabbing your arm and twisting it.

"Ouch," you yell. And into your wide-open mouth, Mr. Watson pours the glass of water.

"Sorry, I don't have time to ask politely, but I want you to drink this formula. Someone has to do it. Now, come over here," Mr. Watson says, and pulls you by the arm over to a mirror on the wall. The two of you look into the mirror and watch as you slowly disappear into thin air. Suddenly Mr. Watson roars with laughter. "I knew I could do it! I've discovered the formula for invisibility!!"

Go to PAGE 52.

The liquid you've clumsily knocked over is rapidly eating its way through the counter top. However, there is one interesting twist: it sounds as though it's humming a pleasant tune as it dissolves the Formica and plywood counter. Terrific. Mr. Watson has discovered acid that entertains. You look for a rag or mop to clean up the mess, and your foot clumsily kicks over a stool, which crashes into a cart, which contains about fifty test tubes, forty-nine of which shatter immediately. You walk over and pick up the one unbroken test tube, but you trip again, clumsily spilling the test tube onto the liquid from the first beaker you knocked over. The combination of chemicals seems to stop the acid from eating through the garage floor, but you've got something more important on your mind. You now know that you're having one of your Clumsy Attacks, something that has happened to you since you were a little kid, and these attacks always come in fours.

Don't bother rereading this page. We'll tell you: you've already done three clumsy things. You'd better just stand there in the middle of the garage without moving for a while. But there is one thing you can do. You can very carefully turn to PAGE 60 and keep reading.

The briefcase contains an inexpensive cassette recorder with a tape of Rory Maltin interviewing someone.

RORY: You say you've known the candidate many years?
MAN: Yes, I've known him since he was a puppy.
RORY: In all of that time, did he ever mention anything about wanting to be president of the United States?
MAN: No, he never said a word about it. He never even said a word!
RORY: And do you think he'll make a good president?
MAN: No, definitely not.
RORY: Why not?
MAN: Well, for one thing, he has fleas.

"That's ridiculous," Titanic sputters. "I've never had fleas in my life. Who would say a thing like that?"

Who indeed? It looks as though you're the only person in the room who realizes that Rory Maltin was speaking to your chemistry teacher and friend, Mr. Watson.

To find out why Mr. Watson spilled the beans, go to PAGE 85.

You are looking at your reflection in a store window, staring at the thick fur all over your face. Foaming saliva is dripping over your fat lips, which open to reveal rows of sharp, white teeth.

"One thing's for sure," you say to yourself. "I'll never succeed on my looks alone." Of course, if you weren't so lost in your own thoughts, you would have also noticed everybody inside the store screaming at the sight of you. Don't they know that beneath this furry exterior beats the heart of a real person, not a werewolf? No, they don't know that and frankly they are not interested. So to prove what a nice wolf you are, you help an old lady across the street, although you end up carrying her after she faints at the sight of you. Then you try to protect some small kids from some big bullies, but you end up carrying all of them to their houses when they faint, too. You even apologize to your principal for not stopping to talk to him earlier, but your wolf breath knocks him cold.

If you're enjoying the fact that everyone is afraid of you, go to PAGE 53.

If you find it annoying, go to PAGE 55.

If this month is September or October, you must go to PAGE 102.

SALE

You try to fight a terrifying werewolf urge, but it's stronger than you are. You don't want to terrorize people in the park; you don't want to scare children in grocery-store carts; you don't want to frighten small animals. BUT . . . you've got fangs, and you have to use them. And just as a thick fur covers your body, a thick anger and hatred of people cover over your good nature during those times when the formula is strongest.

If only you could explain to someone that it's not you, it's the formula making you do terrible things. But no one will listen. For one thing, most people in the town are busy barricading their doors and windows against you. For another, when you do run into people, they spend most of the time screaming instead of listening patiently to you. And then there are the National Guard troops, who have been called out to protect the city. They don't want to listen to you, talk with you, or understand your problem; they just want to shoot you down.

There's only one safe place to hide — at home with your family. But is that really safe? Would you hurt them? Could you *stop* yourself from hurting them?

To find out how your family likes being related to a werewolf, go to PAGE 59.

Everyone on Titanic's campaign team is standing around looking at Rory Maltin's incriminating briefcase as if it were an exotic egg ready to hatch. And everyone wants to do the right thing with it. . . . It's just that there's a difference of opinion about what the right thing is.

"Burn it."

"Sell it."

"Call an exterminator before it spreads."

"No, we've got to give it back without opening it," you insist, picking up the briefcase. You find Rory, catching his breath in the hallway, and return his unopened briefcase.

"Thanks," he says. "I'll do you a favor sometime."

The first favor Rory does is print the scandalous article in the next edition of the *National Filth*, anyway. Good deeds are good deeds, but they don't call it the *National Filth* for nothing.

"Titanic is nothing but a flea-bitten old hound," says neighbor.

In an exclusive interview with the *National Filth,* the next-door neighbor of presidential underdog candidate, Titanic, stated for a fact that the dog has fleas. "That dog has more fleas than my cereal has raisins, and they're probably as big, too." Does America really want a president with two scoops of fleas?

Go on to PAGE 40.

Titanic has a fit and chews the newspaper in half. Then he fires you as his campaign manager because you're too honest for politics.

If you wish you'd never brought your dog with you on this adventure, go back to PAGE 2 and choose again.

Otherwise, go to PAGE 70.

". . . and that's when I left my wife and went back to the CIA for good," Agent Murphy says. He's managed to tell you his whole life story without including one helpful piece of information about how to spot the double agent they suspect exists or how to find Watson's captors.

But you persevere on your own, anyway. For the next couple of days you are the invisible eyes and ears of the CIA, trying to discover the identity of a traitor — someone in the organization who is selling American secrets to anyone who wants to buy them. You select a place where most of the agents hang out, the CIA cafeteria, and you walk from table to table listening for some piece of evidence to nail your man.

"Hey, waiter," one of the agents complains, "there's a bug in my soup."

At another table one of the agents is whispering to the cook. You hurry over there just in time to hear him say, "This pie is delicious. How did you get such a flaky crust?"

"Sorry. That recipe is a secret," the cook whispers back.

Everything and everyone here is a little flaky, you think to yourself as you wander to another table.

Go on to PAGE 42.

"Don't call me Bruce. Call me by my code name," an agent says.

"What's that?" another asks.

"Ralph."

That's right! All of the agents have code names — and what if the double agent's code name is a code name, too!

Lucky for you, this book comes complete with a built-in decoder on PAGE 106. Go there to decode the agents' names. Then turn to PAGE 65.

You burst through the door of Mr. Watson's garage laboratory, forgetting, however, to open the door first. But it doesn't matter. You are not only covered with fur, you're filled with energy and power as well. The formula has changed you into a snarling werewolf. And as you bump into the couple from next door standing in Mr. Watson's driveway, you can tell that you're not exactly the kind of neighbor they had in mind when they moved into the neighborhood.

You take off, running faster than you ever thought you could. You stop a car in the middle of the street and jerk the outside mirror toward your face. The car's driver stops screaming only long enough to faint. Yes, you're a werewolf — no doubt about it. What should you do now? Terrorize? Kill? Devour? Whoops, no time for that. You're almost late for work!

In minutes you're wearing your red chef's hat and apron, standing at your job behind the cash register at Red's Hot Burger Company.

"Is the meat in this burger fresh?" a grumpy customer demands.

"I'll be glad to kill fresh meat for you," you say. It just slips out.

Go on to PAGE 44.

The customer sits down, but she's back at the counter in a minute asking for the manager. "There's a hair in my burger!" she complains this time.

Red, the owner, looks at the burger and then looks at you. "You're fired," he tells you. "You don't meet the dress code. No long hair."

"But my hair is short," you argue. You really need this job.

"Yeah, but it's all over you. You're fired. In fact, I don't want you eating here anymore. Yuch. You're bad for business," Red says, plucking the hair off the hamburger and handing it back to the customer.

You're fired. Pack up and move on to *PAGE 73.*

It's going to be a strange plane flight to California, that's for sure. First of all, Titanic asks for some white wine with his dog biscuit snack. Soon other passengers demand the same thing.

Suddenly a man stands up and yells above the roar of the jets: "I've been on three planes in three days. On the first plane, they served me nacho cheese spread on spinach leaves. On the second plane, they served me chocolate-covered cherries vinaigrette. And now — dog biscuits and white wine. I won't stand for it!"

"You may have red wine, if you'd like, sir," the flight attendant says soothingly to the lunatic, as though he were like any other passenger.

"I don't want red wine. I want some decent food!" the man says, grabbing and twisting the flight attendant's arms and pointing an airline's plastic coffee spoon at her throat. "I'm hijacking this plane to McDonald's, and if anyone tries to stop me, I'll kill her!"

You're about to mention this change of flight plans to Titanic, but he's put a *Do Not Disturb* sign around his neck so he can watch the movie. You figure the news can wait.

If you want to — hey! Are you kidding? Hijackers never give you a choice. Go directly to PAGE 63, or he'll kill her. You heard him.

You head for the university and find Professor Vaccas's office. The door in front of you reads PROFESSOR JULIAN VACCAS, DEPARTMENT OF CHEMISTRY. NO OFFICE HOURS. NO APPOINTMENTS. NO QUESTIONS! DO NOT DISTURB. When you put your hand on the doorknob, an alarm goes off and you get an electric shock that knocks you down. The door opens quickly.

"Can't you read?" barks a frowning face with large, dark eyebrows. The man's eyes seem to burn through you and your friend. "Go away. I'm busy."

"My friend Mr. Watson, the chemistry teacher, sent me here," you explain.

"Oh, no, not again. What is it this time? Pancakes that prevent static electric cling?" he sneers.

You don't like the way this man is making fun of Mr. Watson, but your friend explains what the formula is and how it works.

"Why didn't you say it worked in the first place? Come in! Give it to me," the man says the second the door closes behind you.

"I'm supposed to give it to Professor Vaccas," you say.

Go on to PAGE 47.

"Who do you think I am?" the professor rudely asks, grabbing the small jar of Mr. Watson's formula from your hand. Then Vaccas takes a small, squealing mouse from a cage and rubs a little of the formula on the animal. It disappears in a second. "I don't believe it," the professor says with a loud laugh. "Watson's really done it this time — hahahahaha!"

While the professor is laughing, your friend taps you on your shoulder and points to the mice and guinea pigs in the other cages around the laboratory. They aren't moving, eating, or drinking. They are just staring dully out of their cages.

"Who else knows about this?" Professor Vaccas demands suddenly.

"Just us," you say.

"I'd better take some of your blood to see if the formula has had any bad effects on your system," the professor says, taking a hypodermic needle from a shelf.

If you trust Professor Vaccas, let him take your blood and go to PAGE 78.

If you don't trust him, go to PAGE 80.

"Just think of all the excitement and adventures we can have if we hitchhike to California and go on the *Johnny Carson Show.* It's a dream come true," you say.

"A dream — my aching feet," your dog replies. "There's no way I'm walking anywhere anymore. From now on, I'm not chasing cars — I'm riding in them. And I'll tell you something else: I'm not going to California. I'm going to Washington, D.C. I'm running for president of the United States, and I'm declaring my candidacy right now!"

If you want to help your dog get elected, the campaign starts on PAGE 9.

If you think your dog is barking up the wrong tree, go to PAGE 18.

Quickly you slam the door closed, lock it, and stand in front of it with your arms crossed. "I can't let you do it," you tell your friend.

Just then there's a knock on the door behind you, but no one is there. "You're going to have to be faster than that to stop me," your friend says mockingly from outside the garage.

Think fast. Where is your friend going? What will be the irresistible prize of your friend's first perfect crime? A new home computer? A video tape of *The Invisible Man?* No! You know better than that. It's chocolate eclairs by the mouthful!! You race to the bakery.

Even before you get close enough to the bakery to smell the cookies burning, you hear the unmistakable voice of Mr. Petrie, the owner, working himself up to another heart attack. Mr. Petrie believes everything he touches is a work of art. Unfortunately, Mr. Petrie's hands are not very steady, so he usually botches recipes, and some of his cakes say "Baffy Murfdry, Slorny," regardless of the occasion or the name that should appear on the cake. "Stop, thief!" Mr. Petrie is shouting, as though it were an original thing to say.

Go on to PAGE 50.

Then you hear your friend's laughter next to you! "Don't worry, I saved one for you." Then your friend mushes a fresh chocolate eclair all over your face just as Mr. Petrie runs up to you.

"I've caught you red-handed and chocolate-faced," he says to you. "I hope you go to jail. I hope you get the chair. I hope your face breaks out, you little thief."

"Calm down, Mr. Petrie," you say. "There's a logical explanation for this."

"I can't wait to hear it," your invisible friend whispers in your ear.

If you try to convince Mr. Petrie that your invisible friend stole the eclairs, go to PAGE 66.

If you take the blame and make up a funny excuse, go to PAGE 77.

You've got to get rid of all this fur! Mr. Watson must have a razor around here . . . he's got everything else. A squirt gun filled with cheese . . . a pair of tan shoes with pink shoelaces . . . a panama hat with a purple hatband . . . a book — *One Hundred Useful Things to Do with Dead Batteries* . . . a half-eaten tunafish-bologna sandwich . . . a pogo-stick postage stamp dispenser so you can mail your bills and get plenty of exercise at the same time . . . but no razor!

Sorry, chump. Looks like you've made a bad choice about the razor.

Go back to PAGE 19 and, if you're lucky, *you'll get out of the lab before those people discover you.*

Mr. Watson won't let go of your arm. It's probably turning blue, but you can't see because you are now invisible, clothes and all!

"I'm sorry. I got a little carried away," Mr. Watson apologizes, releasing your arm and sitting down to catch his breath. "My good friend, you don't know it, but you've just done a wonderful thing for science and for your country. And since you're a big part of this experiment now, I'd better tell you something important . . . I'm a scientist working for the CIA."

"You mean the CIA paid you when you invented a roll of cellophane tape so sticky that you couldn't get it off the roll?" you ask.

"All of those failed experiments were my cover so that no one would suspect me. That way I was able to work on top secret projects like this one," Mr. Watson explains.

Just then, the door flies open and two men, armed with guns, move in quickly. They point the guns at Mr. Watson's head. You quickly duck behind a table, but then you remember: they can't see you — you're invisible.

"I guess I wasn't as much of a top secret scientist as I thought," Mr. Watson says, taking off his lab coat and preceding the men out the door.

"Don't talk. Just get in the car," one of the men says.

If you want to call the CIA, go to PAGE 27.

If you want to follow them yourself, get into the car on PAGE 61.

One week and two thousand seven hundred faint victims later, you are once again in Mr. Watson's lab.

"I don't believe my ears," Mr. Watson says, but even though, like yours, his ears are still pointed and furry from the werewolf formula, he means he can't believe what you've just told him. "Maybe you didn't hear me," he tries again, pacing while you sit on a stool and occasionally dab the drool dripping from your wolf lips. "We are human beings; we have feelings, responsibilities, and refrigerators. But right now we look like wolves and everyone is afraid of us, including our refrigerators. But I have finally found the antidote; I have found a potion to turn us back to normal. Now what do you say to that?"

"The same thing I said before," you say. "No, thanks. I'm having too much fun scaring people."

"Sure, that's fun when you're a cub — I mean a kid. But you've got to have a plan, a goal for yourself."

"Okay, try this one on for size: I'm going to Hollywood to star in horror movies. I'll be a millionaire in twelve months."

So you go to Hollywood to star in horror movies, only your prediction isn't completely accurate. Your first flick, *A Werewolf in Dental College,* is an instant smash, and you're a millionaire in six months.

THE END

54

The professor gives you an injection of a fast-acting poison, and you die instantly.

But here's what happens after you die: your friend lasts only thirty seconds longer than you; Mr. Watson accidentally blows up his lab when he forgets how to use his coffee maker; and Professor Vaccas goes on to become the cruelest invisibile tyrant in history.

Maybe next time you won't be in such a hurry to get to

THE END

No one in town speaks to you, your friends run when they see you coming, and soon little kids, growing brave once they realize you are harmless, throw stones and bottles of hair remover at you when your back is turned.

One morning, several long and lonely weeks later, when you wake up, your bed is covered with fur instead of you. The formula has at last worn off, and you look like your old self again. But even though people act as though you've been on a long journey, and they're glad to see you back again, you know that inside you are different. Now you know how it feels to live beyond the city limits of human society, and you feel as though you have a mission in life. So you spend years touring the country and lecturing anyone who will listen on the need for greater sensitivity and understanding for animals, especially threatening ones.

THE END

Wrong! It's not easier to follow an invisibile friend. In fact, it's almost *impossible*.

However, your friend is leaving a trail of a distinctly different nature, a trail you couldn't miss even with a bloodhound with a head cold.

Go on to PAGE 67 and see what we mean. . . .

Well, you're both back home, and it's great to see the old town again — too bad it can't see you. The first person you bump into is Mr. Watson; and because he's still invisible himself, your meeting is more like a head-on collision.

"Ouch! My head. Can't you watch where you're going?" Mr. Watson says. Obviously, he's lost a little of his good humor about being invisible.

"Hi, Mr. Watson," you say. "It's me. Don't you recognize me?"

You and your friend both laugh at the joke, but Mr. Watson sighs with relief.

"Is that you?" Watson says, groping through the air with his hands, although you can't see them.

"Sure," you reply, "and we owe you an apology."

"Yeah, a funny thing happened on our way over to the university — we didn't go!" your friend says. "Hope you're not too mad."

"Mad? I'm thrilled! Professor Vaccas is a killer!" Mr. Watson explains. "I reappeared for a while and went over to see him . . . but that's another story. I'm just glad he didn't get you two first."

"Well, what's next?" you ask, although with Mr. Watson that's not always a safe question.

Go on to PAGE 58.

"Nothing's next. I can't discover an antidote. We've just got to face the fact that we're going to be invisible forever. I thought I was close, but when I gave some of it to my cat, he just grew tap shoes on his feet. He opened the Puss & Boots Dance Academy and is making millions, but I'm still invisible. I've failed."

That doesn't sound like the old Mr. Watson spirit to you, even though it does sound like the voice of reality. You resign yourself to the idea of a blank space above your name in the school yearbook, when Mr. Watson turns to leave. Suddenly you see that the back half of him is visible again. The formula *is* wearing off!

"See you two around," Mr. Watson says. "Whoops, sorry I said that — force of habit."

"That's okay, Mr. Watson," you say with a gigantic, although invisible, grin. "I think you really will!"

THE END

At home, everything at the dinner table is normal so far, except for you, of course, furball.

"I don't understand these kids today," your father says, looking right at you. "Why do you have to wear your hair that way? I can't even see your face."

You try to smile at him, but it comes out as a small snarl.

"Don't talk back to your father. He's had a hard day," your older sister says.

"You call those table manners?" your father demands. "Use a knife and fork . . . and spit out the chicken bones, for heaven's sake. Don't swallow them."

"What did you do in school today, children?" your mother asks, trying to change the subject.

Everything goes along smoothly, until your little brother tries to steal some of your cranberry sauce when you're not looking. You can't help yourself — you bite him.

Suddenly everyone screams.

"Don't worry. There's plenty more cranberry sauce," your mother says.

But the truth is out, and everyone sees it now. You stand up and knock the table over with a small sweep of your powerful arm.

If you want to go out and give yourself up to the National Guard troops, they're waiting for you on PAGE 86.

If you want to keep running, head for PAGE 93.

Uh-oh! You didn't turn the page carefully enough. A swirl of dust specks flies up into your nose, making you sneeze. And when you sneeze . . . you sneeze! (Several archeologists have speculated that one of your sneezes created the Grand Canyon. Their history may be off by centuries, but not their respect for the velocity of your achoo.)

Your sneeze knocks you backward into a shelf of boxes, beakers, and bottles, each filled with a different chemical. You're covered with chemicals of every color and description, and their combined effect is making you very, very sleepy your eyes are getting heavier and heavier . . . you are going to take a long nap . . . and you are going to dream the strangest dream you have ever dreamed (including the night you had a peanut butter and gravy pizza). . . . As the dream begins you've just accidentally drunk an experimental formula of Mr. Watson's, and it's turning you into a werewolf. . . .

Turn to PAGE 38 and dream on!

If the two men with guns had turned around, they would have seen the lab door open and close, apparently by itself. That was you catching up with them. You ride in the empty front seat next to the driver, since the other man sits in back guarding Mr. Watson.

After a while the car pulls up to a crowded drugstore. With you tagging along invisibly, the two men escort Mr. Watson to the back of the store. They shove him through a secret back door. Behind the door is an enormous science lab with every kind of machine and instrument Mr. Watson always said a real lab should have.

You try to give Mr. Watson a sign that you're there, but before you can, another man enters the lab. You can tell by the way the two men get nervous that this new man is the boss.

"Welcome, Mr. Watson, to Operation Rainbow. We think of you, Mr. Watson, as the pot of gold at the end of our rainbow. My name is Raston Von Ranier. I am very easy to work for. The CIA gave you only a garage to work in; I give you the most expensive and complete laboratory anyone could want. All I ask is that you continue your work on the invisibility formula, and you give it to me, not to the CIA. Of course, if those terms are not acceptable . . . I can kill you right now," the man says, never losing the calm, cruel smile on his face.

Go on to PAGE 62.

"I guess I know where I stand," Mr. Watson says. He sounds pretty calm, too, and he goes right to work. The first formula Mr. Watson "tries" fails, and the heavies make a few threats to Mr. Watson. The second one fails on purpose, too, and they threaten him some more. When the third attempt at the invisibility formula fails, one of the men with guns takes off his jacket and says, "This is going to be fun."

It's obvious to everyone in the room that the gunmen are running out of patience. You suspect that speaking up is the only way to stop them from hurting Mr. Watson, but it might endanger you. On the other hand, you look at the chemicals in the room and think that you could start a fire to distract the thugs, while you and Mr. Watson make a getaway.

If you want to speak up, turn to PAGE 81.
If you want to start a fire, go to PAGE 87.

"But we're supposed to be going to Burbank, California," the flight attendant says. "You don't want to make a liar out of the captain, do you?"

"After the food I've eaten, I wouldn't mind making French toast out of the captain. I'm a desperate man and I don't care who I kill!" the man says convincingly.

Just then the captain comes on the intercom and says, "Folks, we'll be landing in Burbank in about ten seconds. I got real busy up here and forgot that I was supposed to tell you ahead of time. Sorry."

The plane comes in for a landing, while hats, coats, luggage, passengers, dog biscuits, and white wine go flying inside the plane. The hijacker is out cold — possibly from starvation.

Titanic wakes up, yawns, stretches, and looks around the plane, saying, "When I'm famous, I'll have to buy my own plane. These public planes look like a dog pound. Well, let's head for the studio. Can't keep Johnny waiting."

In a few hours, you and Titanic are talking to Johnny Carson on coast-to-coast television. It's your first time on TV, and the first time Titanic has been allowed up on a couch. You're nervous but excited, too, because you know that everyone in America is going to see something they've never seen in their lives. First you tell everyone about Mr. Watson's formula and what happened when Titanic drank it.

Go on to PAGE 64.

And then you say, "And he's been talking ever since!"

"Well, I've had guests who were dogs before, but never like this," Johnny says. "How are you feeling tonight, Titanic?"

"Bark," the dog says.

"Very funny, Titanic," you say. "Now say hi to all of the people."

"Bark, bark, bark, bark," the dog says, looking into your eyes.

"Cut out the jokes, Titanic, and say something," you say.

But it's no joke. The formula has worn off, and your talking dog suddenly doesn't have a thing to say. You are disgraced and humiliated in front of millions of people. You die of embarrassment. Johnny goes to a commercial.

THE END

Of course, going through the entire list to decode all of the names was time-consuming; and naturally we put the double agent's name toward the end, but spy work isn't all excitement, adventure, and new, striped knee socks. However, your long-shot gamble has paid off, and now you know the identity of the "traitor." Your next question is what to do with this information.

If you want to follow the double agent and catch him in a traitorous act, go to PAGE 68.

If you want to confront him face to face with the facts, go to PAGE 72.

"The truth is, Mr. Petrie, I didn't steal your eclairs. My friend did," you say.

"What friend? Which one?" he says.

"Well, you can't see him right now," you say.

"I suppose next you're going to tell me your friend is invisible," Mr. Petrie says, wrinkling and pulling on his apron with his nervous hands.

"See, I knew you'd understand, Mr. Petrie. You're terrific," you say with a smile.

"Somebody get a rope! I don't want this one to escape! He's loony!" Mr. Petrie starts shouting again.

Everyone tries to grab you, but your feet are faster, and you run down the street in a blur. You don't have to look back to know you're being chased.

Go to PAGE 67.

Everywhere you look there are crowds outside of stores. Outside the shoe store, there are boxes and boxes of shoes piled everywhere. People are diving and grabbing for them like seals after fish. The bookstore is a shambles, stripped bare because someone put up a sign that said: ALL THE BOOKS YOU CAN CARRY — ONE CENT! And the biggest crowd is around the pet store. Someone has freed all the animals! Dogs, cats, parakeets, mice, guinea pigs, and snakes are walking, flying, and slithering around. The monkey, however, heads straight for the grocery store's produce department, where he pelts with tomatoes anyone who comes near him.

The town is in chaos, and only you know who is responsible, but you don't know what you should do next. You decide to flip a coin.

FLIP A COIN NOW.

If it's heads — go to PAGE 94.
If it's tails — go to PAGE 96.

Following Roberto leads you on a strange, twisty trail. He goes into a bookstore and takes out a book about obedience schools for fish. Suddenly a wall panel slides open and Roberto slips through when no one is looking. You follow him into a brightly lit store with a big sign, The CIA Grocery Store. After buying some groceries, Roberto leaves and goes into a hat store.

"What do you want?" the clerk asks in a strange voice.

Roberto answers him slowly. "I want a hat that's ten sizes too big."

The clerk nods, pushes a button, and a trapdoor in the floor opens up. Roberto goes downstairs (with you tagging along invisibly) into The CIA Laundry where he picks up his shirts. After that he goes into a candy store and buys a whip of black licorice. And when he ties it around his left wrist, a secret door in the back opens up. What now? The CIA Tennis Court? you ask yourself. But you can't believe your eyes when you enter the back room and see Mr. Watson tied up and the two men who kidnapped him nearby.

"Has he talked yet?" Roberto asks the gunmen.

Bingo! Roberto is the one working for the other side!!

Go on to PAGE 69.

"Not yet," one of them answers. "And the Big Man is getting impatient."

"In fact, if he doesn't talk soon, none of you will be working for me very much longer," a voice in the darkness says. The voice moves into the light. When they said the Big Man, they weren't kidding. He must be at least seven and a half feet tall! Still, you think it's a wimpy code name.

"It's time someone cut you down to size, Stretch," you say.

The gunmen and Roberto look around the room trying to see where the voice is coming from.

"Very smart, Mr. Watson. An invisible agent to watch over you. I guess you win this round," the Big Man says, removing the ropes from Mr. Watson.

"I'm going to watch over you, too, Big Man. You'll never know when I'm standing next to you in a secret meeting. You and your friends are out of the spy business for good," you explain.

After you leave with Mr. Watson, word travels fast about the existence of an invisible CIA agent tailing all the other agents. Thanks to you, there are no problems with double agents for years to come.

Of course, no one, except you and Mr. Watson, ever knows that the invisibility formula soon wears off, and that there really is no invisible agent keeping the world at peace after all.

THE END

In November you and your family settle down in front of the TV set to watch your dog, Titanic, and his opponent, Mr. O. C. Buber, debate the issues.

In his summation, Titanic appeals to the public for their votes. "My fellow two- and four-legged Americans: During this campaign I have talked as no other dog running for public office has talked to you before. I've said I want to make America strong; I want to cut taxes, create new jobs, and take a bite out of crime. My opponent has tried to smear me in the newspapers, make fun of me on television, and even sell me to a science lab. Is this the kind of man you want in the White House, or am I the kind of man you want in the White House? I believe the choice is obvious."

Despite O. C. Buber's plea that "if you put a dog in the White House, next there will be owls in the Supreme Court," Americans go to the polls and elect Titanic by a landslide.

During his first four-year term, Titanic works, well, uh, doggedly to keep his campaign promises, and he becomes a very popular president. You keep expecting to hear from him, but you don't get even a postcard. Then one day, three years later, an envelope bearing the presidential seal arrives. Inside there's a form letter asking for campaign contributions for Titanic's next term. And it's not even his real paw print at the bottom of the letter!

THE END

SEAL OF THE PRESIDENT OF THE UNITED STATES

Roberto is sitting in his CIA office when you walk in, invisibly.

"I know who you are, Roberto," you say.

"So Watson really did discover the invisibility formula," Roberto says coolly. Roberto picks up the phone and presses a yellow button on it. A yellow gas sprays Roberto's face, and he falls over dead in seconds.

There goes your chance for saving Mr. Watson. You wonder whether Roberto might have a clue on him. There's a map in his pocket having to do with a meeting! Maybe you'll go to the meeting place yourself.

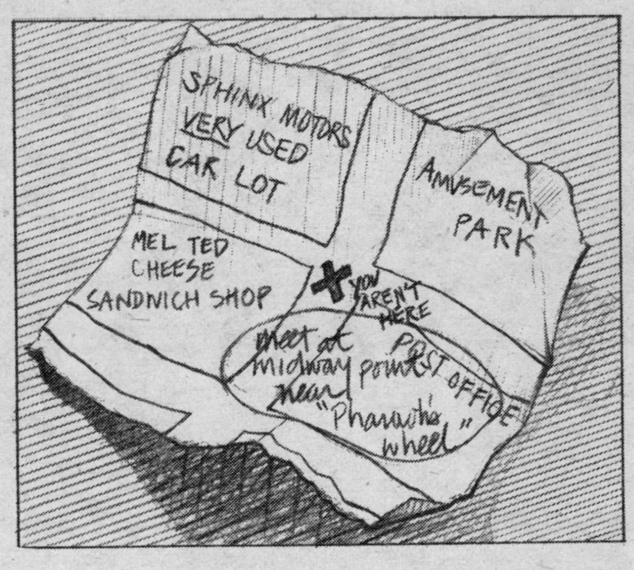

If you go to the midway point, turn to PAGE 31.

You wolf down a couple of burgers and then leave Red's Hot Burger Company for good and head for the library. You need some information about werewolves.

"Pardon me," you say to the librarian, "do you have any books on werewolves?"

"No, all of our books are on paper — ha-hahahaha!" laughs Miss Maffler, the librarian. However, she finally finds a useful book: *Diary of a Happy Werewolf, or I'm Okay and You're in Big Trouble*.

"I forgot my library card," you admit.

"That's okay. You've got an honest face," Miss Maffler says.

You open the book to Chapter 5: "Rules for Happy Werewolf Behavior."

1) Always put a tooth under your pillow at night. If you're a light sleeper, you may get a shot at eating the tooth fairy.

2) Always bite the hand that feeds you.

3) Visit a dentist twice a year. They make useful friends. They also make delicious sandwiches.

4) Never wear white at night because people will see you coming a mile away.

Go on to PAGE 74.

The book also contains chapters on werewolf holidays, wardrobe, and secret werewolf handshakes, plus a vegetarian diet, in which a werewolf eats nothing but vegetarians. The more you read, the more interested you become in becoming a werewolf. You already have the face for it; now all you need are the manners. That's why you're anxious to try out Chapter 11.

Flip to PAGE 76.

"Oh, yeah? Well, two can play at that game," you announce to Titanic as you gulp down some of the potion, unfortunately without considering its effects. You get more than you bargained for! In seconds, you're sniffing the ground, scratching your ears, shaking your head, and acting just like a dog.

"I want to go for a run," you tell Titanic.

"Go chew on a bone," your dog replies, as he tries to order Chinese food over the phone. But because your jumping and barking drive him crazy, Titanic finally says he'll take you out. "I've got to buy some groceries for lunch, anyway," he announces.

On the way to the grocery store, you drive your dog even more crazy by stopping to sniff at everything. Titanic realizes he's made a big mistake bringing you in there.

"I should have tied you up outside," your dog tells you. You race through the aisles of the store, licking the produce and knocking over displays.

"That's it," Titanic says, when he at last drags you out of the store after promising to repay them for the damages you've done. "I've had enough! I don't mind acting like a human, but you're acting just like an animal!"

If you'd like to end your dog days, look for Mr. Watson on PAGE 91.

CHAPTER 11: MAKE NEW FRIENDS BUT EAT THE OLD

> ***RULE #1: Mingle.*** If you want to meet people *you* must go to *them*. If you wait for them to come to you, you'll starve.

You're sitting in the park reading your werewolf book. An old man is trying to feed the pigeons, but they won't come within a mile of him — probably because he's sitting right next to you!

> ***RULE #2: Be Chatty.*** Make small talk. Telling people you want to eat their liver is not a good conversation opener.

"I see you're reading a book about werewolves," the old man says to you first. "Back in my day, that's when we really had werewolves. You didn't have to read about them. They were everywhere. I once found two of them under my bed. Boy, those were the days . . . werewolves thick as flies."

A half-crazy person — who would miss him? You'd miss him! you decide, throwing your book away. He's lonely, and he needs people . . . just like you. You don't want to be a werewolf anymore. You want to be in control of yourself and not at the mercy of Mr. Watson's formula or the full moon.

Go on to PAGE 93.

"The truth is, Mr. Petrie, I'm a sleepwalker, so I must have wandered into your bakery," you say, trying the first thing you think of.

"And ate two dozen of my exquisite eclairs?" Mr. Petrie demands.

"Well, you work up an appetite after all that walking. Besides," you say, licking a little chocolate off your mouth, "there's a little too much sugar in the icing, Mr. Petrie."

If there's one thing Mr. Petrie hates more than someone stealing his pastries, it's someone criticizing them. While he defends himself to the crowd of curious customers, you run from the bakery.

Where is your friend, you wonder, when you see the door to the bank open and close all by itself. You run into the bank, calling your friend's name and begging your friend not to rob this bank.

However, later, when the police arrive, it's your face that appears on the cameras in the bank and your face all of the witnesses describe and identify. And after the trial, it's your face that's behind bars, where you rot in jail trying to convince people that you have an invisible friend, and you were just trying to prevent the holdup.

THE END

"Let's get out of here," your friend says, when the professor is finished with you and his back is turned. "He didn't take your blood — he gave you an injection of something!!"

"Very observant," the professor says, returning with another syringe. "I guess I'll have to take care of both of you."

"Come on," your friend says to you, backing up toward the door.

But suddenly your feet feel like concrete, your legs feel like rubber, and you can't move.

"I always knew that idiot Watson would stumble onto some discovery," Vaccas says, following your friend around the room in no particular hurry. "That's why I encouraged his silly experiments all these years. But I never expected him to discover something like this. Just think of the possibilities. I'll be able to go anywhere invisibly. I can listen to the most private conversations — but blackmailing will be only a hobby. I'll take whatever I want! No one and nothing will be safe from me. I'll rule the world!!" Vaccas says, unable to conceal his crazy, but childlike glee.

You want to stop him, but you're fading fast.

"Run!" you tell your friend. The last thing you see before you lose consciousness is your friend tugging on the locked doorknob as Professor Vaccas closes in with his syringe.

If you're in a hurry to get to the end of this story, rush to PAGE 54.

Apparently having never heard the expression "too much of a good thing," you and your friend continue your invisible journeys. However, the next time you shop in a department store after it's closed, the night watchman accidentally hits you in the knee with his stick; when you try to ride a plane for free there are no empty seats, and you have to dodge back and forth through the aisles trying to avoid the food carts; and when you invisibly crash the backstage at a rock concert, guard dogs sniff you out and chase you for miles.

Worn out by all the excitement of being invisible and on the run, you and your friend devise a new plan. You both go back to your hometown, adopt the dullest kid you can find, and you spend your time following his dull but normal life, invisibly.

THE END

"No, thanks, professor. I don't really want you to take my blood," you say, backing away from him.

"And since we didn't *drink* the formula, it wouldn't be in our bloodstreams, anyway," your friend adds convincingly.

"Don't be ridiculous. I'm not really going to take your blood. I'm going to get you two pests out of my way. Hahaha!" the professor says, grabbing you by your sleeve. But you pull so hard, your sleeve rips off in his hands. Your friend is tugging on the door. It's locked.

You pick up an empty beaker and throw it at the professor. The impact knocks the jar of formula out of his hand. You make a dive for it.

"Give that to me!" the professor orders. "You don't know what to do with it. But I do — I'm going to take over the world!"

You swing and kick at the professor. In your struggle, the jar opens, and thc formula sprays out. Suddenly there is no Professor Vaccas, but his voice is everywhere. "It works!" he shouts. "Now nothing can stop me!" You watch the door open and, just as quickly, close again. You and your friend look at each other, realizing you have just set a maniac loose on the world.

The professor is heading for Mr. Watson's lab on PAGE 101. Follow him!

"Don't touch Mr. Watson, or you'll regret it," you say, sounding tough.

"Who said that?" one of the thugs demands.

"Sounded like a kid to me," the other thug says.

"Shut up, you fools," Von Ranier orders. "Don't you realize we have company . . . invisible company? Mr. Watson's young friend, if I'm not mistaken."

"That's right. Now get away from Mr. Watson, or I'll take care of all of you," you say. You run around the room, knocking things off tables faster than the thugs can turn their heads.

"Okay, okay, stop knocking things over. This stuff costs money and even I have to be budget-conscious," Von Ranier says. "I'll let you go."

"Come on, Mr. Watson," you say.

Watson pushes the thugs out of his way and joins you at the door.

"I congratulate you, Watson," Von Ranier says. "Not only are you a better scientist than I thought, but you're smarter, too. I'll have to be smarter myself next time we meet."

Go on to PAGE 82.

Suddenly you notice that Mr. Watson's face has changed from relief to panic. His eyes are wide, his mouth is open, and he's looking straight at you.

"What's wrong?" you ask.

"I can see you. The formula's worn off!" he says.

"Forget what I said about your being smart," Von Ranier says. "Squash those worms!" he yells to his thugs.

This is your lucky day. We'll get rid of Von Ranier and his thugs. Now go to the nearest phone and call the CIA on PAGE 27.

However, if you want to talk your way out of this mess, go to PAGE 7.

If you wish you'd never started this book, go ask your parents to give you some chores.

Since it's still daytime, you have time to work out a plan. When the captors come back, Mr. Watson will hide under the lab table. He'll do all of the talking, but they won't be able to see him. You'll do all of the moving, but they won't be able to see you, either.

When night falls, five short, fat, black-haired, ugly men enter the lab. You're standing where Mr. Watson was standing, and you're pouring liquids into beakers, but of course they can't see you; only the beakers move in midair.

"Well, gentlemen, I told you I could do it," Mr. Watson says from under the table.

The leader of the group, "Lonesome Doggie" Nelson, can't believe his eyes. "Like, wow! Look at him — I mean, I can't. He's invisible."

"Here, try some," Mr. Watson says, as you hold out beakers for them to drink. Well, maybe they're good at kidnapping CIA scientists, but these guys are also born suckers for a practical joke. They drink the liquid you give them and immediately fall on the ground in a deep sleep.

"They'll be out for about an hour," Mr. Watson says, standing up from behind the table. "That should give my boss enough time to get over here and haul them away. And I've got something here for you to drink, too."

"I hope it's something to make me visible again," you say.

Go on to PAGE 84.

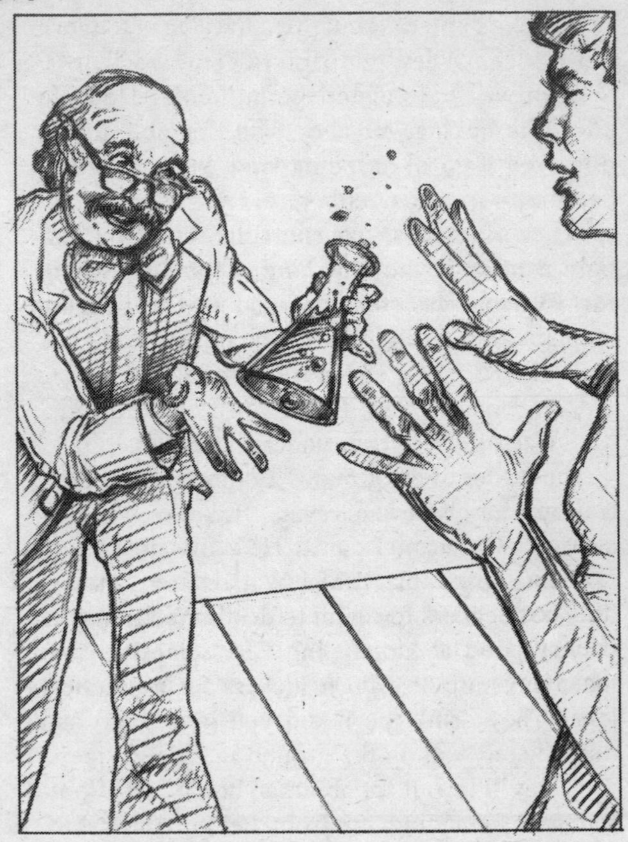

"It is, but if you don't want to try it, you could drink some of this: my latest discovery — one swallow, and you'll not only be visible, you'll be able to fly. Take a sip," Mr. Watson urges.

"No, thanks, Mr. Watson," you answer. "Just give me back my old visible self. I'll take the flying lessons later."

THE END

Right you are about Mr. Watson. You may not know much about highway zodiac signs or even about the comparative gestation periods for the African and Indian elephants (and if you *do* know all about these things and want to put this book down and go back to the encyclopedia, we'll understand), but you sure do know Mr. Watson. He has a very good reason for making his slanderous remarks about Titanic, which he explains to you the minute you arrive at his lab.

"Listen," Mr. Watson begins, "the formula is unstable."

"What does that mean?" you interrupt, not to be rude but just so you'll have something to say on this page.

"What I mean is, right now the formula allows Titanic to speak, and in fact, deliver some of the most eloquent political speeches since Patrick Henry. But at any moment, the formula could change, and Titanic could become mean, vicious, and dangerous. In other words, Titanic could become an animal."

"But Titanic is an animal already," you remind Mr. Watson.

You've got a predicament on your hands. Your dog, a presidential candidate, may be a walking time bomb of viciousness and terror. What next?

To see how Titanic's presidential campaign turns out, turn to PAGE 97.

86

How could I have done that? you think to yourself as you run out of the house, looking for the National Guard and certain death. But maybe it's all for the best. After all, you *are* a werewolf, and you *did* bite your little brother . . . and for what? For trying to steal a spoonful of cranberry sauce!

You decide to give yourself up peacefully to the National Guard, but it's too late. The sounds of booted footsteps and of rifles being cocked snap you out of your thoughts as you stare into the barrels of thirty rifles aimed at you.

Slowly you raise your hands and give up. That's when you notice it. . . .

"Ready! Aim!" the Guard captain shouts.

"Wait!!" you howl. "Look," you say, pointing at the back of your right hand. The fur is fading away, and your skin is becoming smooth and clean again. The formula is wearing off.

You have a lot of explaining to do, but everyone is happy to have you — the *real* you — back once again.

Your life quickly returns to normal, and your hometown unlocks its doors.

One day, the telephone rings for you. It's Mr. Watson. "I've really done it this time," he says. "You'd better get over here as fast as you can."

Again? So soon? After what happened the last time??? So what! You're on your bike in a flash, trying again to break the world's speed record between your house and his.

THE END

The small fire you start does exactly what you expected it to do: Von Ranier and his two bruisers release Mr. Watson the second they smell smoke and run out of the room. But there is an unexpected development: they lock the door behind them, leaving you and Mr. Watson either to put out the fire or pretend you're marshmallows.

"We'd better do something fast," you say. "I may be invisible, but I don't think I'm fireproof."

"I thought you were here," Mr. Watson says. "Thanks for following me. Don't worry. This is just a small fire. I'll take care of it."

Mr. Watson tosses some chemicals on the fire, which instantly bursts into a big fire — no, better make that a major fire. Well, he said he'd take care of it; he never said he'd put it out.

"We're going to die; we're going to die!" you say over and over, as though you were practicing to say it perfectly.

"I've got a plan," Mr. Watson says.

"No more plans," you shout.

"It's a great idea!" he insists.

"If it's anything like the last one, I'll bet it's a really hot idea," you say, futilely throwing a glass of water on the blaze.

Go to PAGE 88.

"I think you should at least hear what it is," Mr. Watson says, coughing a little in the smoke.

"Okay, okay, it'll pass the time," you say finally.

"Why don't we use the fire extinguishers?" Mr. Watson says.

"Great idea!" you say.

You each grab a fire extinguisher off the wall and put the fire out in a minute. Smokey the Bear couldn't have done it better. As the smoke clears, you and Mr. Watson take a deep breath and smile at each other. That's when the telephone rings.

If you want to answer it, go to PAGE 92.

If you want to walk out while it's still ringing, go to PAGE 98.

Unfortunately, Titanic knows the punch line to this old joke, too.

"Don't get many dogs in here?" Titanic says. "At these prices, I'll bet you don't!"

"Hey, kid," the waiter says to you, "why don't you teach your dog how to roll over or fetch — something useful instead of telling old jokes?"

"What do they call a dog that falls off the Eiffel Tower? A French puddle!" Titanic says.

"On second thought, kid," the waiter says, "teach the dog to play dead. His jokes are awful."

"Hey, will you shut up? We're listening to the dog," someone in the ice cream shop calls out.

Suddenly Titanic is on his feet, his back feet, that is, walking around the shop. "But seriously, folks, human beings are interesting. Take my master . . . please! You know, a man came up to me the other day and said he hadn't had a bite in three weeks. So I bought him lunch! Hahahahahaha!"

The people in the ice cream shop are howling, but you're annoyed.

Go on to PAGE 90.

"Titanic, we get the idea. Give it a rest for a while. It's time to go home," you say.

"Don't you understand? I *am* home. For the first time in my life I know who I really am. All my life I've been a comedian trapped in the body of a dog. Now I have the one thing I've been missing," Titanic says.

"Bad jokes?" the waiter says.

"Now I have a voice. Listen to those people laugh. My audience loves me!!"

When you look around the room, you notice for the first time that the place is packed and people are still trying to squeeze in, a fact that does not go unnoticed by the shop owner.

"I'll give you two hundred dollars a week — two shows a night and all the butterscotch-and-marshmallow sundaes you want," the owner says, holding out her hand to Titanic.

"What do you call a dog that gives piggyback rides to foxes?" Titanic asks. "A fox *carrier.*"

And what do you call a dog that tells jokes? An overnight sensation. And loyal to his master to the end, Titanic sends you a postcard from every city he plays in. Big deal.

THE END

You follow Titanic back to Mr. Watson's lab, stopping a couple of times along the way to growl menacingly at some cats in the neighborhood. The cats think you're teasing, but their owners think you've lost a few marbles. Twelve people call your parents to complain; two of them call the dogcatcher.

When you arrive at the lab, you and Titanic find Mr. Watson there. The biggest surprise is seeing the red rubber ball he's carrying in his mouth. "You know, this formula makes me feel as playful as a pup," Mr. Watson says, rolling on the floor to scratch his back.

"If you drink enough of it, it'll make you feel like chasing cars," Titanic says, and you bark your approval at the idea. But come to think of it, that red rubber ball looks pretty good to you. You try to grab it away from Mr. Watson, but he snarls at you.

"Okay, you two, listen up," Titanic shouts at the two of you. "Until this ridiculous formula wears off, you're going to have to learn how to get along with each other. So the first thing you'd better learn is how to *sit*. After that I'll teach you *heel,* and maybe even roll over, if you learn quickly."

The formula never wears off. Fortunately you and Mr. Watson are fast learners, and soon Titanic is entering you in dog shows all over the country. You and Mr. Watson keep walking off with the top prizes in obedience!

THE END

Who can resist a ringing telephone? It might be the CIA calling to say they've captured Von Ranier just as he was about to leave the country. Or it might be Von Ranier calling to see if you made it out of the fire alive or toasted. Or, worse yet, it could be your mom reminding you that you have to babysit tonight for your cousin. Are you sure you made the right choice?

Too late for second thoughts, you pick up the phone and say hello.

"Howdy, pardner," says a loud voice at the other end. "This is Jerry Jeff John at WQQQ-FM, the radio station that wants to put some excitement in your life. And just for answering the phone we've got a fabulous, exciting, free gift for you. It's an all-expense-paid tour for you and your guest through our city post office. But hold onto your hat, pardner, because that's not all. We're also sending you a certificate for a free vanilla milkshake — how about that?"

"Would you call the police, the fire department, and the CIA, please? There has been an attempted murder, a kidnapping; the place is crawling with spies; and we just put out a fire," you say, when you finally get a word in.

"You kids certainly say the darndest things, all right. What an imagination! Well, forget the prizes, punk. I guess you don't want a little excitement in your life," Jerry Jeff John says and hangs up quickly.

Right.

THE END

Uh-oh . . . there's a full, white moon tonight. It's your night to howl!! And you take it literally because you start screaming and baying at the moon as if daring it to answer you back.

Suddenly you do hear an answer — another howl in the distance. Was it the moon? Someone trying on designer jeans two sizes too small? You follow the sound of the howling, and it leads you straight to Mr. Watson's laboratory!

Inside there's a werewolf just like you, except that it's wearing a starched and pressed white lab coat. You realize immediately that it's Mr. Watson hard at work trying to find a cure, an antidote, confident that if science could beat the frizzies it certainly could cure the furries.

Mr. Watson takes a sniff of the potion he's mixing in the beaker. He coughs, he gags, he chokes, he sneezes, and then he adds a little salt and hands it to you.

There are four things to consider before drinking this new potion. The first is Mr. Watson's track record for successful discoveries; and the other three really don't matter after that. Well, do you think this antidote will work?

If so, take a slurp and turn to PAGE 95.

If not, don't drink, don't spill it, but carefully and slowly turn to PAGE 99. Who knows. The whole book could explode in your hands!

OR

If you want an ending sent in to us by Jenny Arthur of Worthington, Ohio, turn to PAGE 110.

You never find your friend again, or Mr. Watson, either, who, knowing him, may still be sitting in the movie theater trying to scheme up a daring plan for getting soda out of the machine without paying.

But every time you hear about a politician sitting down on a cream pie, or read about volcano alerts in Chicago, or any other crazy prank or mysterious event . . . you just figure it's your friend striking another blow for illogical explanations . . . and having a *great* time doing it!

THE END

Mistake with a capital M! Some people never learn.

Watson's antidote turns you into a five-foot-tall Princess telephone. "Whoops, wrong number," Mr. Watson says and hands you another antidote.

He keeps mixing them, and you keep taking them. The second one turns you back to you, only your head is on backward — great for horror movies, but bad for walking, wearing ski parkas, and playing basketball. The third turns you into a crybaby (the less said the better).

By the seventh antidote you're an ostrich in a football helmet, and you've got to decide whether to try number eight or go stick your head in the sand somewhere.

"I've failed," Mr. Watson says. "At this point, I don't think I could make a bowl of cereal right."

"Are you kidding? I'm having a great time," you announce, much to his surprise.

Pretty soon, Mr. Watson's antidotes turn you into something you do like, and reporters from everywhere rush to your town to see the only walking, talking piece of red licorice in captivity.

THE END

You're in Mr. Watson's lab again. You were hoping he would be there, but all you find is a note in his handwriting.

> I've come to the conclusion that there is no antidote. Being invisible has its drawbacks. People keep sitting on me on buses. I'm going off by myself. I always pictured us working on experiments together. I was even going to buy you your own accident insurance policy. But now . . . well, best of luck.
>
> Watson

"Doesn't give me much to look forward to, does it?" your friend says.

"What are you doing here?" you ask.

"Probably the same thing you are: looking for something to turn me visible again," your friend says. "Wouldn't you know, the first thing Mr. Watson does that works, works too well."

"I thought you were having a great time," you say.

"I did for a while," your friend says. "Now I don't know what to do. I'm not going home. I can't. My parents couldn't stand the shock. It would be like living in a freak show. The novelty and the fun wear off pretty fast — even for me."

To see how things work out for your friend, turn to PAGE 109.

If you think your friend should go home, go to PAGE 100.

During the next months of the campaign, you keep the terrible secret that the formula, which has helped make Titanic a candidate for the presidency, could at any moment also make him a candidate for the electric chair. But you keep the secret to yourself because you don't want to believe it, and you know that Titanic won't believe it if you tell him.

The candidate himself has never felt better. Titanic sweeps across the country gathering voters the way a broom gathers dust. In November, the voters overwhelmingly elect Titanic as their next president. Your reaction is happiness mixed with relief.

Inaugural Day is a cold January morning. Titanic looks very impressive in his formal attire, as he stands at the podium and delivers his inaugural address. Many people are close enough to the new president to see the white foam spilling over his lips, but only you know enough to begin shaking at the sight. Suddenly Titanic interrupts his speech to snarl, growl, and bare his teeth at the crowd.

However, no one thinks this behavior is the least bit unusual, and so Titanic serves his full four-year term. Years later, the history books say that during this period, America had a president whose bite was just as bad as his bark.

THE END

The phone keeps ringing, but you don't answer it.

"I've had enough adventure for one day," you say.

"It's the CIA," Mr. Watson says. "I wear a radar device, so I'm sure they're calling to say they're on the way."

The two of you leave the burnt-out lab and walk into the phony drugstore. There are cops everywhere, and most of them are pointing guns at Von Ranier. A man in a trench coat comes up to Mr. Watson and says, "Good work, Agent Watson."

"What are you doing here so fast?" Mr. Watson says.

"We've been here for hours," the man says.

"Then who's that on the phone?" Mr. Watson asks.

You don't know and what's more, you don't care. Spies, formulas, guns, agents — phooey! You just want to go home and give your dog a nice, quiet shower.

THE END

You don't want to hurt Mr. Watson's feelings, so you remind him that his shoelace is untied. And since he spends most of his life in his lab or in the classroom instead of watching *Happy Days* reruns, he falls for the old joke immediately. While he bends down to tie his shoes, even though in his present werewolfian state he couldn't fit a shoe on his paw if he wanted to, you quickly spice up the potion, adding a few ingredients of your own. Certainly it can't hurt.

You drink the potion, and suddenly the lights go out. Either the potion is working, or Mr. Watson forgot to pay the electric bill again. When you open your eyes, you are your old self again; and so is Mr. Watson! *Your* formula cures you!

THE END

Well, it's true that your friend comes from a pretty straight family. Their idea of doing something daring is pouring ketchup on their French fries. Your friend's father sets an example of rigid honesty — he's so honest he wouldn't steal third in a baseball game. And he and his wife firmly believe in the old maxim that children should be seen and not heard. This latest development would definitely blow their minds.

So you convince your friend the best thing to do is to write them a "good-bye, I'm running away" note, then live secretly with you so your friend won't be totally lonely. And even though your parents accuse you of having a tapeworm because your appetite has doubled, and of being a little weird because they hear you talking and laughing to yourself in your room, everything works out fine in

THE END

You and your friend arrive outside Mr. Watson's garage laboratory and try to run in, but something holds you back. Suddenly the entire garage explodes in an enormous ball of fire. And when the smoke clears, there's nothing there but a large hole in the ground.

Then someone taps you on the shoulder. You turn, but there's no one there.

"It's Vaccas! Run!" your friend says.

"Relax, you two," says the friendly voice of Mr. Watson. "There isn't enough of Professor Vaccas left to put on a small cracker. I followed you to his lab today and, when I saw what was happening, I raced back here and changed my notes. When Vaccas tried to mix up some more formula, he really found out what invisibility is all about!"

"But *you're* still invisible. Where's the antidote?" you ask.

"I *knew* I left something in the lab!" Mr. Watson says, kicking dirt into the hole in his backyard. "Hey, you two don't have a garage your family isn't using for a while, do you?"

THE END

You run at top speed to Mr. Watson's garage, trying hard to remember not to run on all fours. You've suddenly thought of an idea so wonderful it makes you laugh till you howl, an idea so simple that it only took a look at the calendar to think of it. Luckily you find your furry teacher in his lab rather than in his den.

"We are sitting on a gold mine," you tell Mr. Watson, panting heavily.

"The way this formula backfired, we're lucky we're not sitting on fat, bushy tails," Mr. Watson says unhappily. He's been taking this latest invention pretty hard, especially since his wife is suing him for divorce and, to add insult to injury, she has hired a lawyer from the ASPCA.

"What do most people do during October?" you ask.

"Most people enjoy the fall colors and nippy weather. You and I will probably have to search for a place to hibernate," he says.

"Wrong! Most people look for an original, one-of-a-kind Halloween costume, something authentic and natural-looking," you say, smoothing the fur on your snout. "Your formula is an instant Halloween costume, Mr. Watson!" you shout, jumping up and down and howling for joy.

Go on to PAGE 103.

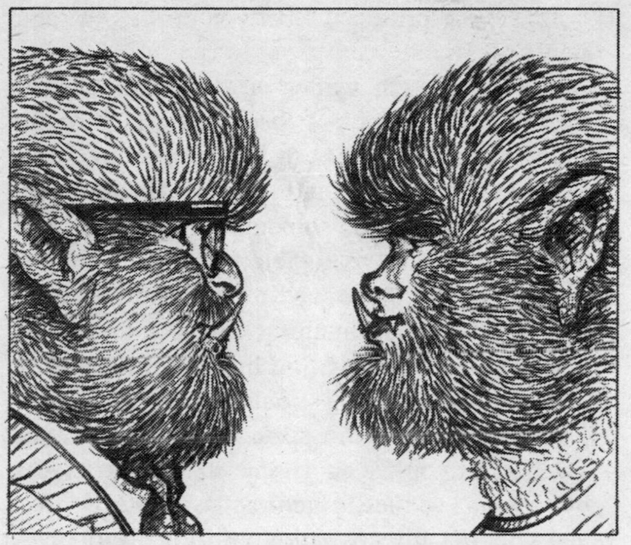

More than that, it's an instant success. You and Mr. Watson, as president and vice-president of the Hair Raising Research Labs, Inc., forget to inform your customers of the *permanent* qualities of the formula you sell and become millionaires in a week. And when Mr. Watson finally comes up with an antidote that will reverse the formula and reduce the werewolf population to its former, manageable size, you become multimillionaires.

THE END

"At these prices, I'll bet you don't," Titanic says.

Apparently the waiter is as unfamiliar with this old joke as you are, because he falls on the floor laughing and has to be carried out of the store to catch his breath and regain his composure. Meanwhile, someone else comes over and sits down at your table.

"Excuse me," she says. "I couldn't help overhearing that man laughing like a baboon over that old joke your dog told him. With talent like that, you and your dog should go on television."

"You mean on the six o'clock news?" you ask her, as you watch Titanic struggling to pick up a spoon and then forgetting the whole business and sticking his nose directly into the sundae.

"No, I mean on the *Johnny Carson Show.* You could make a pile of money. I have a brother who lives in California. I'm sure he could get you on the show if he tried." The woman goes directly to a pay phone and starts giving the operator orders as if the world were coming to an end. You look at Titanic and wonder if maybe it has.

Go on to PAGE 105.

"I've always admired the ice cream delicacies of this establishment," Titanic says, licking his lips. "Not that you would ever share one with me. But I'm more generous. You may lick my bowl if you want."

"He wants to talk to you," the woman says. You stand up. "No, you!" she says, pointing to Titanic, instead.

Titanic clears his throat and speaks into the phone, "Hello. How are you? How's your hot tub?"

"Isn't that wonderful?" the woman says to her brother, taking back the phone. Then her face drops and she hangs up. "He didn't believe it was really you. Says he has to see it with his own eyes first. You've got to go to California immediately."

If you want to take a plane to California, go to PAGE 45.

If you'd rather hitchhike, turn to PAGE 48.

THE CODE

SPECIAL FOR ALL SPIES COMING FROM PAGE 42: Decode all the agents' names in the list below. Some of them will spell out gobbledygook, and some will spell out words. Then you'll know who the double agent is.

To decode the agents' names, here's what to do. Find the letters of each name in the top row of the code (marked with *). Change each letter to the one beneath it. For example, UTLM spells CODE.

*A	B	C	D	E	F	G	H	I	J	K	L	M	N	O	P	Q
S	A	Q	Y	I	N	V	W	Z	P	J	D	E	U	R	G	K

R	S	T	U	V	W	X	Y	Z*
T	H	O	C	L	F	X	M	B

AGENTS' NAMES

Marvin
Arnold
Ralph
Diane
Gail
Alexandra
Roberto
Murphy

When you have found out who the double agent is, go to PAGE 65.

Well, it seemed like a good idea at the time, you think to yourself, as Von Ranier and his two thugs watch with barely concealed smirks as you raise the beaker to your lips. Closing your eyes, you take a sip. Then you smile at everyone.

"Swallow it," Von Ranier says. He must be watching closer than you think.

There's something familiar about the taste of the thick, syrupy liquid, and you try to remember what it is. What is it? Mr. Watson's candy-flavored rat poison, developed so that the little rodents would at least die with smiles on their faces? No! No! Suddenly you know what what it is! It can't be! you practically scream out loud when you realize that, luckily, you have just taken a swig of one of Mr. Watson's diet colas. He drinks a million of them a day and never cleans them out of the beakers when he's done! This discovery is going to make dying a lot easier for you, because it will be completely fake! You clutch your throat and spin around, screaming as though you were on fire. Then you fall down on your back and lie there like a piece of uncooked bacon. Pretending you're almost dead, you struggle to raise your head and tell Mr. Watson, "Whatever you do, don't drink it."

Go on to PAGE 108.

This, of course, is immediately taken as an open invitation for Von Ranier's guys to open Mr. Watson's mouth and pour the liquid in. But there's one problem: Mr. Watson doesn't know enough to pretend to die, so he just stands there. When no one is looking, however, you raise your head again and wink at Mr. Watson and, seeing that you're all right, he falls to the ground immediately.

After Von Ranier and the two thugs leave, Mr. Watson calls the CIA. "Well, I have new orders," he says, after hanging up. "I have to leave town immediately and find somewhere else to work. You've been my best assistant as well as a good friend, and I'm going to miss you."

He shakes your hand, walks out of the lab, and you never see him again. But every year on your birthday, you receive cards with no signature and no return address. And because the cards quack like ducks when you put them in water, you figure Mr. Watson still remembers you.

THE END

"There's less to this invisibility business than meets the eye," your friend says to you.

In a little while you're watching bottles and beakers and powders float by in midair, as your friend tries to find the antidote.

You can't see your friend's hand, but you can see what's in it . . . a glass filled with a bubbling, churning liquid.

"Are you really going to drink that?" you ask.

"I guess so," your friend says and gulps the liquid down.

Suddenly there's a scream that shakes the windows and, when you open your eyes, your friend is standing there good as new.

You stare at each other for a second, and you ask, "Do you know who I am?"

"Why? Have you forgotten?" your friend asks and explodes with laughter, pounding you on your back as though you were choking. "That's a good one, huh? Let's go — I can't wait to tell everyone I got you with that one." Well, your friend is back, *stronger* than ever . . . only to you it seems like someone who just looks like your friend. Guess the antidote had some bugs in it. Well, maybe Mr. Watson can work on it. On second thought, Mr. Watson may turn your friend into a gorilla. So you forget about calling him and settle for a friend who's as strong as a gorilla and has the sense of humor of a chimpanzee!

THE END

110

Dear Authors,

Here is my ending:

Your faith in Mr. Watson is justified, because his antidote changes you both back to yourselves. You're really happy and decide to hurry out of the lab to tell everyone the good news.

When you open the door you discover that the National Guard troops, thinking they have caught two werewolves at last, have surrounded the lab. They shoot the minute the door opens, blowing away you and Mr. Watson for good.

THE END

Dear Jenny,

You have a sick outlook on life. Do your parents know you send endings like this to authors?

Dear Readers,

Don't blame us — blame Jenny. It's getting so that we're afraid to open our mail these days.